For my lovely family.

A.B.

For Aria, Lorenzo, Enzio, Loretta and Leah.

S.M.

EGMONT

We bring stories to life

First published in Great Britain 2019 by Egmont UK Limited,
The Yellow Building, 1 Nicholas Road, London W11 4AN
www.egmont.co.uk

Text copyright © Anne Booth 2019
Illustrations copyright © Sarah Massini 2019

Anne Booth and Sarah Massini have asserted their moral rights.

ISBN 978 1 4052 9082 1

A CIP catalogue record for this title is available from the British Library.

Little Cloud

Anne Booth

Illustrated by Sarah Massini

EGMONT

ONCE there was
a dream of a cloud,
waiting, hiding,
in a blue sky,

which became
a whisper of white

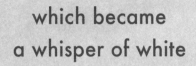

and grew and grew . . .

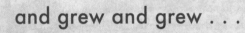

Until there it was,
a little white cloud.

"Here I am!" said the little cloud.

"What a beautiful little white cloud," everybody said.

And the little cloud felt very proud.

"Look at me!"
the little white cloud said.

And they did.

"It looks like a ship," they said.

"It looks like a baby."

"It looks like a dog."

"It looks like a bone."

Everybody loved looking at the cloud making all sorts of shapes for them.

And the little cloud loved making shapes for everybody.

But as time went on it got bigger and darker and heavier.

"Look at me!" said the cloud.
"Look what I'm doing!"

And everybody said . . .

"Oh no, it's raining!"

And they put up their umbrellas and ran away!

"Where are you going? Come back!"
said the cloud, as it began
to rain more and more.

Because raining is what
rain clouds do and that
is what the little cloud
had become.

"Why aren't you looking at me any more?
Aren't I clever, raining like this?"

And it grumbled and rumbled.
And stamped and flashed.

"Nobody is glad to see me any more,"
cried the cloud, sadly.

"I am!" said a little flower, stretching out its leaves for a drink.

"I am!" said a farmer, watching the rain help his thirsty plants to grow.

"Really?" said the cloud,
feeling a little better.

And it kept raining, because
that's what rain clouds do.

"We're happy to see you," said the fishes,
swimming in the water . . .

that was filling
the streams,

which were flowing
to the river,

which was flowing
to the sea.

"We are," said the children
splashing in puddles.

"Really?" said the cloud, happily.

"YES!" they cried.

So the rain cloud rained and rained
and rained and rained.

And then . . .

. . . the sun came out and took the last of
the raindrops, and made them into a rainbow.

After the rain, the birds sang in a sky washed clear bright blue again.

And the grass was green, plants sprouted in the gardens and the fields, and flowers turned their faces to the sun.

And the cloud wasn't
a rain cloud anymore,

but a little white
cloud again,

which the sun tickled
into a whisper of white

and back into a happy dream of a cloud again,
waiting and hiding in a blue sky.

Until the next time . . .

Because sometimes, raining is what
a little rain cloud has to do.